My "h" Sound Box®

WRITTEN BY JANE BELK MONCURE • ILLUSTRATED BY REBECCA THORNBURGH

E
MON

The Child's World®
childsworld.com

Published by The Child's World®
1980 Lookout Drive • Mankato, MN 56003-1705
800-599-READ • www.childsworld.com

ISBN HARDCOVER: 9781503823112
ISBN PAPERBACK: 9781503831339
LCCN: 2017960310

Printed in the United States of America
PA02371

A NOTE TO PARENTS AND EDUCATORS:

Magic moon machines and five fat frogs are just a few of
the fun things you can share with children by reading books
with them. Reading aloud helps children in so many ways!
It introduces them to new words, motivates them to develop
their own reading skills, and expands their attention span
and listening abilities. So it's important to find time each day
to share a book or two . . . or three!

As you read with young children, you can help develop
their understanding of how print works by talking about the
parts of the book—the cover, the title, the illustrations, and the
words that tell the story. As you read, use your finger to point
to each word, modeling a gentle sweep from left to right.

Simple word games help develop important prereading
skills, including an understanding of rhyme and alliteration
(when words share the same beginning sound, such as "six"
and "sand"). Try playing with words from a book you've
just shared: "What other words start with the same sound
as moon?" "Cat and hat, do those words rhyme?" The
possibilities are endless—and so are the rewards!

My "h" Sound Box®

Little 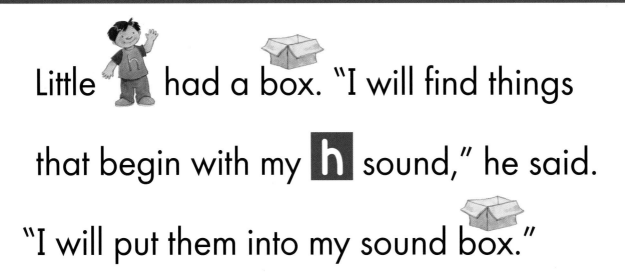 had a box. "I will find things

that begin with my **h** sound," he said.

"I will put them into my sound box."

He found some hats.

He put a hat on his head. Did he put

the other hats into the box? He did.

Little  found a hen.

"Hello," he said. "I need a hen for my sound box." He put the hen into the box with the hats.

Then he found a hog. Did he put the hog into the box with the hen and the hats? He did.

Little  found a horse. He was

happy. He hopped on the horse.

He rode the horse up a high hill.

"I want to go higher," said Little . But the horse

could not go higher. They were on top of the hill.

So Little  put the horse into the box

with the hats, the hen, and the hog.

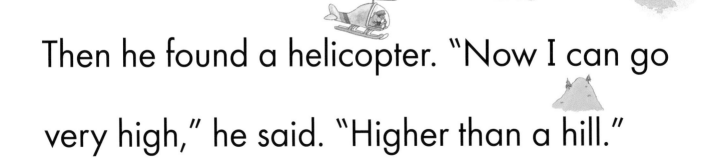

Then he found a helicopter. "Now I can go

very high," he said. "Higher than a hill."

The helicopter went so high that the hen,

the hog, and the horse cried, "Help! Help!"

So Little h put the helicopter into the box.

Now the box was heavy. Little  put it
on his head. He did not see the hole.

He hopped into the hole. "Help! Help!"

"How can we get out of this hole?"
asked the hen, the hog, and the horse.

Little  had a horn. "I will blow my horn," he said. He blew the horn.

A hippopotamus heard the horn.

He helped them out of the hole.

"Hooray for the hippo!" everyone hollered.

"How can I thank you for helping us out of the hole?" asked Little .

"You can take me for a ride in the helicopter," said the hippopotamus.

So Little  took the helicopter out of the box. He and all the animals went for a ride.

They flew over a highway, over a hill, and

all the way home.

There, Little  spread out his things.

My! How many he had!

Little h's Word List

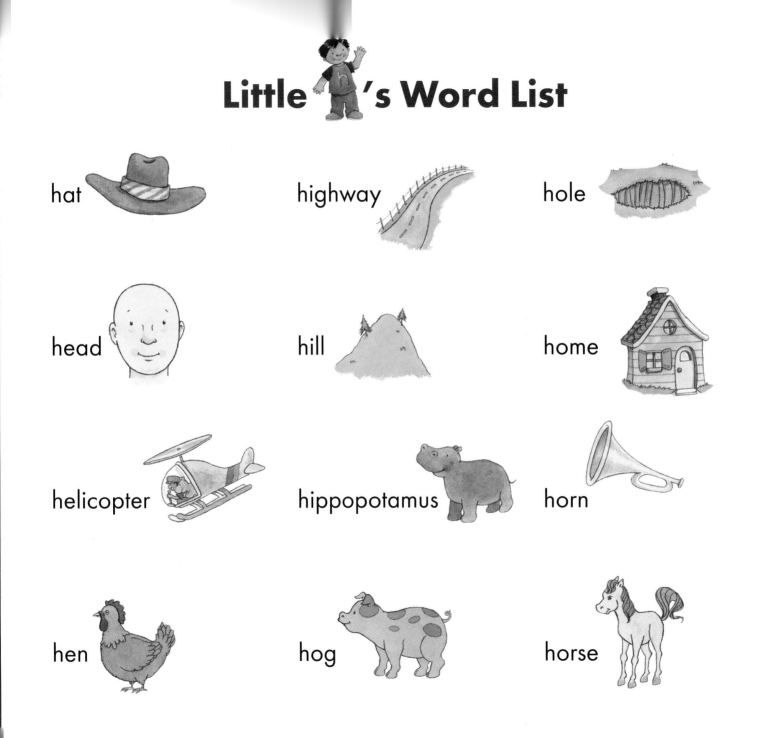

hat

highway

hole

head

hill

home

helicopter

hippopotamus

horn

hen

hog

horse

Other Words with Little

hair

harp

hood

hamburger

heart

hospital

hammer

hive

hot dog

hand

honey

hummingbird

More to Do!

Little  put hats in his box. You can collect hats, too!

Directions:

Look around your house and gather all the hats you find.

1. Sort the hats according to color. How many red hats do you have? How many purple hats do you have?

2. Sort the hats according to size. How many big hats do you have? How many little hats do you have?

3. Do you think the hippo, the horse, the hen, and the hog would each like to wear a hat? Which of your hats would they put on their heads?

Just For Fun!

Gather some paper and crayons. Then draw a picture of a hippo, a horse, a hen, or a hog wearing one of your hats.

About the Author

Best-selling author Jane Belk Moncure (1926–2013) wrote more than 300 books throughout her teaching and writing career. After earning a master's degree in early childhood education from Columbia University, she became one of the pioneers in that field. In 1956, she helped form the Virginia Association for Early Childhood Education, which established the first statewide standards for teachers of young children.

Inspired by her work in the classroom, Mrs. Moncure's books became standards in primary education, and her name was recognized across the country. Her success was reflected not only in her books' popularity with parents, children, and educators, but also by numerous awards, including the 1984 C. S. Lewis Gold Medal Award.

About the Illustrator

Rebecca Thornburgh lives in a pleasantly spooky old house in Philadelphia. If she's not at her drawing table, she's reading—or singing with her band, called Reckless Amateurs. Rebecca has one husband, two daughters, and two silly dogs.